# Song of Middle C

## Alison McGhee
### ILLUSTRATED BY Scott Menchin

CANDLEWICK PRESS

First edition 2009

Library of Congress Cataloging-in-Publication Data is available.

Library of Congress Catalog Card Number 2008934176

ISBN 978-0-7636-3013-3

2  4  6  8  10  9  7  5  3  1

Printed in China

This book was typeset in Kosmik Bold.
The illustrations were drawn with pen and ink and colored digitally.

Candlewick Press
99 Dover Street
Somerville, Massachusetts 02144

visit us at www.candlewick.com

For Kari Dondelinger Luoma
A. M.

For my mother
S. M.

Do you play the piano?
I do. And next week is my first piano recital!

"Practice makes perfect,"
says my mother.

Hoo boy! Don't I know it! I practice all the time.

I've practiced so much that I've lost track of time.

Great artists often do, you know.

Haydn, Mozart, Beethoven, Bach—
they all lost track of time.
That's what Miss Kari, my piano
teacher, tells me. And she
would know.

My recital piece is called "Dance of the Wood Elves." I know it by heart. That's because of all my practicing.

Hoo boy, have I been practicing!

Miss Kari says that I bring great imagination to my musical interpretation.

Miss Kari says that true artistry
*requires* great imagination.
When I play "Dance of the Wood Elves,"
I imagine the wood elves dancing.

Those wood elves sure love to dance.

On the day of the recital, I wear my lucky hat.
And my lucky shoes.
Not to mention my lucky underwear.
Nothing wrong with good luck, I say.

This is what true artists do at the end of their
recital pieces: Bow. *Clap.* Bow. *Clap.*

"My baby!" says my father. *"Magnifico!"*
"You'll be the hit of the recital!" says my mother.

That's not what my big brother says.

"You might be wearing your lucky hat," says my big brother. "But can you take the heat?"

Of course I can!

"And you might be wearing your lucky shoes," says my big brother. "But when push comes to shove, are you as cool as a cucumber?"

Of course I am!

My big brother doesn't know about my lucky underwear. And I'm not about to tell him.

At the recital, I wait and wait and wait.

Did you know that piano recitals take a long, long time? Especially when your song is the very last song on the program.

The very, very last song.

But am I nervous?
Hoo boy, no!
Not one tiny bit.

That's because I'm cool as a cucumber.

My turn? Already?

Fingers in position. Thumbs on middle C.

A one, and a two, and a—

A one, and a two, and a—

Fingers? Hello?
Wood elves, where are you?
Lucky underwear, don't fail me now!

Fingers back into position.
Thumbs on middle C.

**Oops!**
Didn't mean to do that.
That is not how "Dance of the Wood Elves" begins.
Hoo boy, no!

Yet middle C is a very distinctive note.
That's what Miss Kari says.
There's only one thing to do.

I play it like a question.

I play it like tiny wood elves who have lost their lucky underwear.

And I finish with a long sustain.

It was certainly not the recital piece I had practiced for.

But I stand up and bow anyway.

"I had no idea that middle C had such range," says my mother.

*"Splendissimo!"* says my father.
"My baby, an improvisational genius!"

"You forgot your piece, didn't you?" whispers my big brother.

"What a fascinating composition," a man with a mustache says. "What do you call it?"

"That piece is brand-new," I say. "It's called 'Song of Middle C.'"

I look at Miss Kari. She looks at me.

"True artistry requires great imagination," says Miss Kari. "And great improvisation."

And, just in case, lucky underwear.
Hoo boy!